Towards a parliament for cats

by four-legged Louis
and two-legged Geoffrey Hooper

First published in the UK by Inglenook Press
70 Fitzalan Street, London, SE11 6QU

First edition published 2020

Text © Geoffrey Hooper, 2020
Illustrations © Harley Bishop, 2020
The author and artist have asserted their rights to be identified
as the originators of this work in accordance with the
Copyright Designs and Patents Act 1988

ISBN: 978-1-71688-371-2
Imprint: Lulu.com

A CIP catalogue record of this book is available
from the British Library

Design by Martin Parker at silbercow.co.uk

Acknowledgements
Thanks to Martin Parker for his excellent advice and expertise in the design
and layout of this book. Thanks to Harley Bishop for his delightful
cartoons. My love and appreciation to my wife Wendy for her patience
and comments on the book; also to the comments and suggestions from
our children, Louisa, Fraser and Theo. And remembering with affection
four-legged Puku, Puki, Sammy, Smutty, Whisky and Louis.

To order more copies turn to: https://bit.ly/2Y9r9FF

... I'm a North London cat – London Borough of Barnet (West) to be precise. I'm grateful to Geoff for his help with this book. He's not a bad chap – a writer of course, a retired journalist in fact and a friend to cats. He and his missus have been married for over 50 years and they've had three children but, more to the point, they've looked after six cats in that time. Our book not only talks about our rights but I've managed to make him see life from a cat's point of view. So anyone lucky enough to be sharing their home with a cat – or anyone else of course – may find something to smile about, even laugh out loud, especially children or parents reading this book to their children. Not only that but there's the story of Lavender Isle and how I met the lovely Minnie. She's quite tiny with lovely white fur. Tell you more later!

Contents

1

On our rights and being hard done by

L ife is not all tum-tickling for cats. Roll over pussy and have your tum tickled, there's a good pussy. Okay, so I like some tum-tickling from time to time. It hits at my comfort zone and allows me not to think of my self-esteem for a moment, nor dignity as I luxuriate in the sensuality of prone tum-tickling, the supine position being best. But for a cat who is not just some bum moggy who never even bothers to trim his whiskers, there is more.

Nowadays, being a trim-whiskered cat implies certain responsibilities, obligations, rights and duties. Being a trim-whiskered cat means being on your toes, fast on the prowl, claws sharp – and I mean not just sharp but razor sharp, honed on stone – so you can take out the living room curtains in just one swipe. Obviously, I'm talking here about cats who live with humans – that is to say, old Two-Legs – not maverick cats, go-it-aloners, or back-alley bruisers all belly-aching, brawling and no brains.

Trouble is, in society, we're bottom of the list. Of rights, we have none. We are disenfranchised. That means we can't vote. There are no votes for cats. That is why I am beginning this consciousness-raising campaign, working towards a Parliament for Cats. For we are not merely miaow-machines, tender on the tactile; we are not just moggies, four-legged, friendly, furry and cute; we are feline fellahs and fellarinas, guys and dolls with brains, hopes and ambitions. We have our dreams. Mine are not just about going to Lavender Isle (tell you about that later) but for a full parliament of cats, all seats filled after being duly contested, so we can begin the true democratisation of the feline kingdom. Let's fight for the rights of moggies!

2

For England and St George!

For our parliament to be successful, we need to embrace all British cats – and by British cats, I mean those living in the British islands, whether they are Siamese, Persian, Manx, Devon Rex or Sky-Blue-Pink moggies. The only requirement needed is that they sniff the British air, prowl the British land and, be they high-born or low-born, cats in kitchens or cats in castles, cats in cities or cats in the country, pedigree cats or kaleidoscopic cats with the benefit of a diverse lineage – such as in my own distinguished case (a jumble sale of genes, my mum always said) – the only qualification is that they consider themselves to be part of that great constituency which is the Great British feline nation. It would not be jingoistic to declare that it is the finest in the world. There is more intelligence, more variety, more skill and talent within British cat-hood than anywhere else on Earth. Much of this success is a tribute to the British cat lover. The story does not end there, however, for it is the united campaign of British moggies throughout the land that has moulded the British character into the deepening realisation of the need for a cat in their life and thereby promoted their ever-widening interest and – it would not be too much to say – feline dependence. Perhaps that needs to be said loud and clear: the British are dependent on their feline friends. The Brits have been moggie-ised! And it is to our credit that we have brought such a situation about.

There was a time when a cat thought of little else but his territory, his love life, his grub, his proper ration of tum tickles. In other words, a perfectly understandable agenda of personal satisfaction. However, with the introduction of our regional charm centres, with many day and evening classes for moggies, as well as some roof-top workshops, many cats, and indeed I would dare to say most, have come to realise that when they lay on their back, paws in the air, abdomen in the exposed position, ready and waiting for tum-tickling to commence, that it is not just for themselves that they assume this position but for England and St George – by which, of course, I mean the UK.

For England and St George!

3

On relations
with Two-Legs

The mister and the missus I am staying with (temporarily, of course, until I get a place of my own) are okay. Why should there not be some good Two-Legs around? They are called George and Betty and they feed me from tins and I can let myself out into the back garden through the cat-flap. I choose, however, to go out of the front door, particularly first thing in the morning when they have to unlock it and rush about in search of keys while I sit patiently licking my lips and whiskers after a good breakfast.

I'm a city cat, North London to be precise, Barnet (West), high on the hill, on the outer edge of London to be even more precise. So, I'm not some country cousin living under a haystack whose only pleasure is the feral yapping at the fetlock of some horse or cow, but an urban feline, urban and urbane, a cultivated creature, a bit swanky and suave, if I say so myself.

Going out the front door brings me into the street where they start parking their cars as soon as business hours begin. Sometimes I sit under one of the cars or else I stroll into a parking space so some motorcar driver has to honk his horn to get me to run off before he or she can park. Usually, I don't run off. Sometimes, if I've had a good night and perhaps signed up a lot of new members, I jump on to the bonnet. Although in comparison to this heavy metal car I'm quite tiny, not even half the size of one wheel, and much less the size of a Two-Legs, this can frighten them a lot. They tremble and go all shivery. Oh! Ah! That cat! Sometimes I'll sit there or sometimes I jump off and walk away with nonchalant disdain, all bare-bottom and couldn't-care-less. A bit posy, of course, but we need every artifice at our disposal.

Sometimes I jump on the bonnet

I could walk away with my tail swinging slowly from side to side but that implies anger. I could hold my tail straight, like an arrow but that is a bit unrelaxed, as if you've just been electrocuted. I prefer the arch and loop position and I pride myself on being blessed with a tail long enough to effect this stance of extreme indifference. All you do is curl the tail up and over your back, the emphasis being on the regularity of the curve. It focuses the bare bottom and is very nonchalant. I like it. Some hosts, by which I mean that abominable term 'cat owner', which is not only insulting but inaccurate because you can't own a cat, you can only graciously allow a cat to live with you, some hosts object to our bare bottoms as something not very nice. If it were up to them, they would design a little flap to be worn over our bald behinds, just as the Scots people sport a sporran on their kilt. But our bare-flesh buttocks, our fur-less rumps, our unzipped rears are a pointer to reality. We wear them with pride. As they say in pubs: 'Bottoms up!'

Feline dependency

All the time we have to bear in mind our so-called feline dependency. Perhaps it has gone too far. Some of my colleagues think it has. They are considering guerrilla tactics to shake up moggy complacency. They are the members of the BRCB – the British Radical Cats Brigade or alternatively and perhaps better still, the FLM – Front-Line Moggies. Some of their suggestions involve more of what you might call armchair violence, that is to say, more mayhem on carpets, curtains and three-piece suites. This would mean a work-to-rule campaign, such as: Thursday midnight, slash the curtains; Monday morning, three-piece suite.

It has to be gauged just right because otherwise you could get slung out, which goes to show how vulnerable we are: no rights of domesticity. The object is to make the hosts fully aware of, and responsive to, our existence, not to take us for granted; and to stir up complacent moggies into action.

There is also the fiery group, a bit over the top, mostly short-haired ginger tigers, who call themselves the CTOB – the Catakazi Tin-Opening Brigade. Their leader is a volcanic one-eared, much scarred tortoiseshell called Bisto who thinks he's God's gift to cats. Always making speeches. Always about to march on the supermarkets and raid the cat-food shelves. Claims he is working on a tin-opening method that doesn't need a tin-opener.

So, we have to admit an uneasy dependency. But isn't old Two-Legs dependent too?

Warfare on carpets, curtains and three-piece suites

4

Names for cats

My mother named me Louis after my Uncle Bob (a mystery I never understood but then my mother could be very forgetful, especially after eight kittens – I think most of us were called Louis after Uncle Bob).

Talking of names, at number 45 Birchwood Gardens, in the London Borough of Barnet (West), high on the hill, where we live, there is a moggy called Nelson. He is black and white with a black patch over one eye, just like Nelson, says his mister and missus. The rest of his face is white. My friend Barnabus, the barber-shop cat who lives in the barber's shop in the high street, and who seems to know everything, even if half of what he knows isn't true, my friend Barnabus tells me that Nelson was a famous English sailor who won the battle of Waterloo Station in London when the Spanish Armada sailed up the Thames. He lost an arm and an eye in the scrum. Apparently, it's very crowded there, especially in the rush hour.

Barnabus said that Nelson was also part of a love triangle. I asked Barnabus what sort of triangle was that and he thought it was what he called an i-sausages triangle. He didn't say whether that was pork sausages, frankfurters or chipolatas. I like sausages and hamburgers. I don't think Nelson would have been partial to a hamburger.

Undermine feline dignity

The cat next door, whom I don't really like because he's such a snob, is called Flim-Flam. Not a very flattering name. In the cul-de-sac in Barnet (West) where I lodge, there are twelve cats and about a hundred houses. Many of the twelve have names which undermine feline dignity. A name might be appropriate when you're a kitten, a bit scatty and cuddly, but when you are a hardened warrior, victor of a hundred roof-top maulings, and scarred on face and limb, your tail tip long since bitten off in the struggle for supremacy, then it can be irksome and demeaning to the self-esteem to be called Knickerbocker. It's hard to be top gun if you're sitting there surrounded adoringly by some young lady cats – and I've had my fair share of that, I can tell you – and you are recounting some passing triumph against a dozen unneutered ginger moggies, when your missus person comes to the front door and starts cooing. 'Co-ee, co-ee. Are you there, Knickers? Din-dins, Knickerbocker!' I ask you! It's more than a cat can bear.

One of our resident cats is a fine Burmese, bit of a wise old bird, not getting any younger now, of course. I

A Zest for Life is packed full of colourful, energising recipes, made with ingredients that taste great and also help you to feel great!

These fresh and tasty recipes will make eating well effortless as they are easy to prepare and absolutely delicious.

With superfoods galore and meals that keep you full for longer, this collection of clever, nutritious recipes is one that you'll turn to time and again.

Here, you'll find all the recipes you need for a healthy lifestyle throughout the year, in one beautiful cookbook.

- BOUNTIFUL BREAKFASTS
- PACKED LUNCHES
- AFTERNOON SNACKS
- WEEKDAY MEALS
- WEEKEND SPECIALS

A Zest for Life is a high quality hardback cookbook, printed in full colour. Size: 205 x 275mm (8 x 10¾").

79 easy to follow triple-tested recipes ● Inspiring photo for every recipe ● Nutritional information ● Cook's tips

---

FRESH, TASTY RECIPES THAT WILL PUT A SPRING IN YOUR STRIDE!

This book is packed full of colourful, energising recipes, made with ingredients that taste great and also help you to feel great!

don't bother him myself but some of the younger cats go to him for advice: management problems mainly, usually to do with our hosts not carrying out our wishes, not doing what we tell them; and some personal relationship problems with other cats – break-ups, re-groupings, changing partners, what shall we do with the kittens? – and of course, problems concerning self-esteem: where am I on the scale of pampered puss at one end and murderous moggy at the other? Are my whiskers at utmost trim? Is my coat too glossy or not glossy enough? So he knows a thing or two, if a bit pompous.

Such a cat should be called something dignified, such as Solomon or Eustace, as befits an old gentleman who now likes to spend a lot of his time sleeping. In the afternoon when it's sunny his favourite place is on the roof of our next door neighbour's shed. He's getting a bit stiff, particularly in his back legs, but he can still haul himself up our laurel tree and on to the fence, a scramble made easier because the tree slopes at the bottom. He wobbles unsteadily along the fence, narrow as the width of my tail, until he can jump on to the sloping roof of the shed. He curls up, nose to tail and closes his eyes and goes to sleep.

Such a peaceful picture of genteel dozing in the afternoon sun – his black, white and grey coat making him look lawyer-like and distinguished – should be complemented by a gentle calling to wake him from his slumbers. Instead, his missus, a vulgar woman, shouts in a voice so harsh it's like two tin roofs being rubbed together: 'Wake up, Lollipop!' No sensitivity at all. And what a name for such a cat! No respect for such a fine feline fellow.

5

Feline folklore

Among the middle classes, and particularly those who read those long newspapers, there is a fashion to give pet moggies soppy names, as if there is a point-scoring game in operation with more points for so-called wit and soppiness. There is a young cat down the road at 26 – the Edwards family – very light on her paws, dainty when she eats, a good posture when she sits. Her mister and missus don't know it yet but she's caught a good few mice. She wanted to take one into the house as a gift and a trophy. Who wouldn't be proud of a good dead mouse?

But when she came to see me one night I advised against it. Two-Legs aren't always appreciative of dead mice. Several times in a fit of enthusiasm after a successful hunt, I've taken dead mice into the house and laid them carefully on the carpet in the living room. Mrs Two-Legs comes down in the morning and there are shrieks of 'You naughty cat!' – no gratitude at all. Then she goes barmy with a cloth and disinfectant and the mouse is wrapped up and thrown into the dustbin. I try and hang around to explain in my own sort of way but the mood she's in it's not a good idea and I allow her to chase me out. Usually I go and sit in the laurel tree to give her time to feel guilty.

Anyway, some of this feline folklore I have been passing on to this sparky girl at 26. I wouldn't say her coat is ginger but I wouldn't say it wasn't, more a light shade of marmalade with a pretty stripe as if she were wearing a stripy jumper. So she's pretty and dainty, so why call her Postlethwaite, just to be all fancy, and shorten it to Postle?

Anyway, I'll call her Poppy because, well, we'll see... Not that I'm interested, of course, but when I know that she's in her garden in the evenings, I might just jump over the fence, say hallo... Makes me think of Lavender Isle. (Tell you more later.)

6

Food for felines

Nowadays tinned food is what we eat most. We used to be self-sufficient, of course, catching our own, just as tall Two-Legs used to do. So far, we have not started using knives and forks to eat our food. It certainly saves on the washing up and we get along nicely without, thank you very much. You could argue that it would be neater and tidier if we could have some sort of clip-on handles to make it easier to hold a knife and fork with our front paws. (We wouldn't need knives or forks for our back paws.) Of course, we should need a table and chairs and a tablecloth. Naturally, being the only cat in the family, I would be eating at my table alone, unless I had friends in. They would have had to take knife-and-fork training as well as know something of table manners. These vary, of course, from place to place, particularly in places where they don't have tables. If we were to introduce table manners for cats, we would need to draw up a code of preferred practice.

Should we use whisker protectors when supping soup? And would it be good manners or bad manners when eating a kipper to add a tad of mustard to your kipper with your tail? Lots to sort out.

We would also need to be clear about DIY grub. Is it an inalienable right, to be enshrined in a constitution for moggies, to hunt mice? Do we need a referendum? At times of increasing awareness of rights for Two-Legs and four-legs and animals, do we need to recognise the inalienable right of the mouse not to be hunted? There has to be a bit of give and take in all this. If me and my chums are to forgo a choice morsel of rump-of-

OK to add some mustard with your tail?

mouse steak then the National Federation of Mice would have to stop – or ration – their members from eating cheese and pickles, or fish and chips – or whatever their diet is. Trouble is, no-one is going to open a tin for a mouse. You'd have to go a long way to find a supermarket with tinned mouse food on its shelves.

That leads me to say that if our proposed parliament were to vote to increase our hunting, and we budgeted for increased training in bird recognition and mouse life-style, as well as optimum methods of catch and surprise, it could impact heavily not only on the aforesaid, that is the birds and mice, but also the tinned cat food industry. We should need a very clear head on whether we wished to invade the economy in such a manner. And were our Parliament of Cats to take merely a feline view, saying, in effect, let the UK economy go hang – what has it go to do with us? – then I would have to say that such a parliament would not be a British Parliament of Cats but little more than a bunch of scratchers, squeakers and

Is it our right to hunt mice?

squawkers. To be counted, to be worthy of inclusion, to be trusted, to be respected, to be able to hold our heads up, whiskers trim, claws sharp and tails of a certain sprightliness, we must be ready as a parliament of cats to take our place, to serve the nation, to maintain standards, to pass on traditions to our fellow felines, such as for example, a bit of late-night knees-up caterwauling from time to time.

Dreaming of fish

That's what I dream of, when I'm not dreaming of fish. Recently, I have dreamt of nothing but kippers and dipping a paw into a fast-running stream to flip a fish on to the bank. But in Barnet (West), high on the hill, sadly, they don't have such streams.

But talking of dreams, I happened to hop over the fence the other night and chatted to Poppy, asked her if she wanted to help with the campaign fighting for the rights for moggies. She said: 'Why don't you ask Minnie?'

'Who's Minnie?' I asked, 'She's coming later,' Poppy told me while curling her long tail over her pretty ears. 'You might be able to help her with her problem.'

So that's how I first met Minnie in the garden one summer's evening.

My 'Egyptian' stance

7

A note on posture

If you put your front paws straight out and sit on your haunches, a neat and powerful curve to the back, head straight, whiskers parallel or with a slight upwards rake as is permitted in a gentlemanly cat, then you have adopted the posture which I call the Egyptian stance in recognition of the classical pose of cats in Egyptian statues. It is a pose I adopt when I am feeling cool, when there is nothing on my mind. Perhaps I've taken a prowl around the house, a bit of a slinky lope around the street and reconnoitred the garden, doing a bit of leaping in the air after a butterfly or a bird, or just leaping; or perhaps a full frontal assault on a bush, which means going slightly berserk in the undergrowth as if I were doing to death Georgie, the boxer dog next door.

He is something of a smug dog, goes for 'walkies' with his master or mistress and wears a red bow at Christmas. Right twit he is! Sometimes, when I can hardly be bothered to chase him - you have to be a little choosy whom you chase for the sake of your reputation – sometimes I just stroll across his lawn. He barks – more a honk than a bark – a proper honker he is – then I race up their cherry tree. He barks at the bottom of the tree – can't climb it of course! – getting very excited and wagging his stump of a tail from side to side so fast that I wonder it doesn't either drop off or take off. Then he'd be an even more bare-bottomed boxer. The only thing more pompous than him are his folk, his missus and mister. They are mega-pompous. I mean giga-pompous. One of these days I'll climb their lace curtains and swing about a bit. Then they'll squawk and Georgie Boy will bark.

One reason why I even bother with him is because his barking sets off the pampered poodle on the corner. He doesn't go walkies or anywhere except hide under the table. He yaps when Georgie Boy barks. I think it's good for him. So making Georgie Boy bark, the poor old thing, is really therapy for the pampered Poodle. My good deed. His missus and mister are having him psychoanalysed. No wonder he hides under the table. He has a block, say his missus and mister, about barking. A bit of a woof-less wimp, if you ask me. Some tree climbing and jumping from roof to roof, combat style, guerrilla mode, would do him good, though he'd probably slide off the tiles. His fur's all curly. He'd probably slide off on his curls. Perhaps next time I'm passing the corner I'll go out of my way to growl at him if he's around – see if that makes him bark and shout.

Sometimes Two-Legs notice that felines stare. We might sit in a corner and stare or stare at a wall or a tree. This behaviour is partly rest, partly an adoption of an internal posture so that you can re-align your energies, and partly for watching out for what you might call the invisible humans, although they are not so much humans as angels. Sometimes on a special day they will pick you up and give you a ride to the stars and back. They would make you invisible first, of course, so you didn't catch cold, and so's Two-Legs wouldn't notice. There's also a special place to go to, which is a secret I might share if I'm in the mood, post-kipper consumption perhaps. Always puts me in a good mood.

Why can't humans see angels?

I've never understood why most humans can't see angels. My mother used to say it was because humans played the violin and didn't always look one another in the eye, though I don't think that not looking into one another's eye referred to when they were playing the violin, although it could have, if my mother was right. She had eight kittens in several years and she had to answer lots of kitten questions so that I think she had a store of answers to questions and sometimes got mixed up and gave the wrong answer to a question. If you asked how long is a cat's tail she would say as long as a piece of string and sometimes say it's right under your nose. She also used the last bit to answer the question: where is the universe? Right under your nose, she'd say, or right under your tail.

We would be told off for biting each other's tails when we were kittens. You've only got one coat, she'd say, you mustn't spoil it, particularly your tail. Can't send your coat to the cleaners. You can tell a well-bred cat, she'd say, particularly when she was showing us how to do our morning wash, you can tell a well-bred cat by its tail. Don't try to stand on your tail like a ballet dancer or swing on it from a lamp or a branch of a tree, or join tails with another cat to make a skipping rope to jump over, or stiffen it with glue for pole-vaulting over hedges, or apply hair oil to make it posh and smarmy, or slip-on rings for slicing up all the alley-cat moggies in the alley. Tails, she said, not least when she had us all curled up for bedtime, tails were a cat's refinement, to be kept clean and held high. You can't increase its length or furriness. Keep your head up, your whiskers trim and your tail high – particularly when going through doorways.

That was very sound advice. I often enter the house by the back door and then, if Two-Legs are about, I will go to the front door and wait for them to open it. They often say: 'But you've only just come in,' as they open the door. I say to myself: 'But who's in charge here? Me or you?' But I'm careful not to get smug and, although I walk through the doorway slowly, solemnly, to keep them waiting, I keep my tail tall, very tall, tall as a lamp post, so that apart from putting on the dignity, it can't get trapped. So my mother's advice was sound. She taught us all the classic feline postures, handing on the tradition, you might say.

My 'body enclosed by tail' posture

Once we had learned them, she said, we could adopt them or vary them.

I frequently use the 'body enclosed by tail' posture. It looks particularly fetching if you can adopt it while on a cushion – always bearing in mind that the colour of the cushion shouldn't clash with the colour of your coat. Some Two-Legs have little sense of cat-colour co-ordination. Presuming you can find the right cushion, you can turn around two or three times, to the left or the right depending on how you were brought up, and

Your paws are stuck out like railway lines

then curl up in a ball. Your back legs are brought around towards your head and your head usually rests on your two front paws, which are stuck out straight ahead and parallel, like railway lines.

You can turn your head sideways and rest one cheek on your paws or you can settle your chin squarely between your paws looking straight ahead. If you look up at Two-Legs in this position, they sometimes go ga-ga with delight.

Last of all, you move your tail. I can still hear my mother saying: 'And last of all you position your tail.' She had a check list which we had to learn: back legs, front legs, curve of the back, tilt of the head, tilt of the whiskers, and the eyes, open or closed, one eye or two – 'and last of all you position your tail.' So when everything else is in place, and you feel relaxed and properly in posture, then you move your tail, not so much flicking it into place as lifting it and lowering it with a wrap-around motion. Right at the last, it is permissible to flick the very tip of the tail. If you can lay it over your nose, or even seem to be sticking it into your eye, then Two-Legs not only go ga-ga but goo-goo and squeal.

How long is a tail?

Of course, this brings us back to that difficult question of how long should a cat's tail be. The ideal is to be able to adopt the 'body enclosed by the tail' posture with the tail fully enclosing the body and being sufficiently long to overlap the nose, if required. It must be said that not all cats can meet this standard. Some who can't become morose and suffer from whisker droop. This is another area where feline parliamentarians could legislate, either to widen what is the desirable and acceptable standard or to fund tail-lengthening procedures or the purchase of false stick-on tails.

When I was chatting to her the other evening, I discovered that Minnie has a very acceptable tail. I also liked her coat. She is furry white all over, a tiny cat with eyes that look a bit orangey. A tiny cat, as I said, so tiny that when I put my paw out to touch her on the shoulder I was scared of pushing her over. I shouldn't have been scared. She mistook my intention and her paw shot out and bashed me around the ear. I was very abashed, as they say.

8

Our living conditions

For comfort for cats, there is nowhere quite like a well-sprung armchair. Birds have their nests, dogs their kennels, but the modern moggie really prefers a well-upholstered armchair. Certainly there are other places for snoozing, such as on a rug in front of the fire or on a ledge behind a sunny window, but for comfort and protection from draughts you can't beat an armchair that's soft and cosy. It's a snooze palace, particularly if there is a plump cushion at the back of the chair which you can lean against. Also, if you catch a mouse when you go hunting in the early morning you can store it under the chair until you feel peckish. However, I am not always successful in hanging on to it because my house-persons aren't keen on dead mice under the chair and on the carpet in the living room. Often I have been having a late-morning lie-in when the missus, whose name is Betty, will come down for breakfast and start to go potty, waking me up just because there is a bit of a mess in the

They aren't so keen on dead mice under the chair

hall or living room or perhaps the tail of a mouse under the table. I get a bit weary from the way she carries on. 'George,' she shouts, George being her husband. 'George get up quick. He's got a mouse. There's mess everywhere. What shall I do?'

There are some aspects of human nature which a cat can only tolerate by gritting one's teeth, twitching one's whiskers and keeping a tight grip on what would otherwise be a very tetchy tail. You can always tell a feline's temper by the mode of his tail. When it is straight and quivers like one of those arrows just shot into the trunk of a tree, beware. That moggy is in utmost anger mode, maximum moggy maliciousness, fearful feline ferocity. In this mode, his tail is in such a tense electric quiver that if you had the right socket you could plug him into the vacuum cleaner and clean the house.

Perhaps I can empathise with Betty and George about putting the mouse under the chair and perhaps the carpet does go gooey but it can be washed. Anyway, I can't easily open the fridge. It would be different if I could.

One area for investigation and possible legislation is refrigeration for cats. I am not suggesting we need air-conditioning or anything like that but it would be helpful to have cat fridges, which we could easily open. They wouldn't need to be very large. We might keep some herring there or some kippers and the odd mouse or two, perhaps some milk and cream as well as custard. I am not a little partial to custard, especially after those salty kippers. It seems to slip down well and your whiskers retain a custardy odour for an hour or two until it's time for a whisker wash.

My mother was always saying that if you wash your paws every hour, keep your whiskers clean and don't get tempted by dustbins, however enticing, or stay out all night not more than three nights in a week, then you should live a long life. I have proved the truth of this. I know many a haggard moggy who has lost his health, his looks, his whiskers, by burning the candle at both ends. You can't be a roof-top romantic every night, my mother said. You've got to give your hormones a chance. The night-time howler-prowler thinks himself a cute cool cat, with his whiskers clipped, tail a-twinkle with sauciness and spice. Such a high-tile tom was a real flash cat, said my mum with a chuckle, because he was gone in a flash, his libido lost, his whiskers vanquished, his high-class sleekness as limp as a dead daisy.

Lift from an angel

I try to pace myself: snooze time, food time, play time, hunt time, perhaps a bit of stare time. Stare time, as I said, is when you watch the invisibles. Several times I've had a lift from an angel up to the clouds and seen all the sights on Earth below. I have seen the cities and the roads, the rivers and the high places and it's all very nice being such a tourist but what I like best are short trees in the London Borough of Barnet (West), high on the hill. You can climb up short trees; the tall ones are only for bringing in the fire brigade. It's a useful way of asserting yourself, of course, and making the house persons realise how much they love you.

You choose a tall tree that's fairly public, such as a tree in front of the house where you live, and a time when everyone's at home, such as a weekend or a long summer evening, and then you run up the tree and pretend you can't get down. You mew a bit as if you're dying – and a crowd gathers. Then your house persons ring for the fire brigade and a big red engine comes roaring down the street. The crowd gets larger and great big firemen with helmets and axes climb the tree. This is all very frightening but you have to overcome the twitch of your whiskers and let them carry you down. Usually you get tears, cuddles and caviar for three days afterwards – or at least tinned tuna – because they are all so pleased to see you back.

It is important to keep reminding Two-Legs how much they value you. Obviously, this is a difficult area to legislate for. It would be taking things a bit far, perhaps, every time a Two-Legs took on a cat or kitten as a house companion, to have some sort of ceremony or oath-taking in which, in return for purr and fur, the human promised not so much to love honour and obey, which is so much taken for granted that it's hardly worth saying, as to provide full-time access to grub with a bit of tum-tickle thrown in. However, we could institute a form of annual licence which would list the Two-Legs' obligations towards their feline companion. We would not need to define closely the human's tolerance towards our propensity to climb up the curtains nor the frequency with which they should play with their companion or stroke the fur. The wording of the licence would be more of a cats' charter, a delineation of desirable living conditions. For example, we wouldn't want to specify kidneys for breakfast on Tuesdays and haddock for supper on Fridays but there would need to be some declaration as to the quality and frequency of food. One would not want to say that one must have double cream rather than single cream but it would be nice to know that some cream was on the menu, if only twice a week. Similarly, one would not want to be hard and fast about the quality of the blankets or duvet for one's basket. I realise, of course, that not all cats have blankets or baskets, nor indeed do they necessarily want one. However, it is not true to say, as I heard one young cat say (and, mind you, he was a very puffed-up and proud-of-himself cat) that only old or middle-aged cats want a basket. The argument goes that they've lost their cat-hood, that is, their out-on-the-tiles joie-de-vivre, their feline gusto, their moggie elan – and settled instead for the security of basket-hood.

Forty winks on the sofa

This is simply not true! I know many a refined cat who has had a basket since infancy. I certainly would prefer not to be without my basket. If I do take a short snooze, some forty winks on the sofa, or an armchair, or in front of the fire or in the sunshine of a window ledge, I am not forsaking my basket. These are to be thought of as excursions, partly to satisfy the mature mind's need for variety, and partly to be seen to be in domination of my territory. It doesn't do to let Two-Legs off the hook for a minute. Moggies rule supreme, okay? And must be seen to do so. Therefore, a charter for cats could well be an early item on our parliamentary agenda.

Baskets, of course, make me think of Minnie. I asked her if she thought what Two-Legs call my shirt front was as white as her coat, which is very white. She smiled at that and I felt she wasn't angry with me any more. She still has this problem, however. It's sort of getting to be my problem too. There's a favourite spot of mine in the fork of our laurel tree. It can keep me comfortable when I want to sit and think and I seem to be having a lot of thoughts about her and her problem just now.

9

Careful in the manifestation of delight

Of course, in the hot weather I scratch a bit more. Sometimes it's the fleas and sometimes it's the twigs, berries or buds from the garden. She, Mrs Two-Legs that is, doesn't like me scratching.

'Louis, stop scratching,' she says, and wags her forefinger at me as if to menace me – not that she would, of course. She's a softie who tries to tuck me up at night in my basket and will wrap my tail around me and talk to me in baby language.

'There's a good puss, Louis,' she says.

Sometimes I will purr a bit to play the role. Other times I will roll on to my back with my white tum all feather-warm and my paws bent and wimpish, looking up at her between my paws with my head cocked to one side in what she is pleased to call my pirate look. I don't know whether it is my pirate look – whatever that is –

but it seems to work. She kisses the top of my head between my ears, bending low to do so, and with her finger crooked rubs under my left ear. This is quite nice and sometimes I allow myself to purr.

However, you have to be careful in the manifestation of delight. It is a wise cat who knows the balance between macho and marshmallow. You don't want to become one of those continuously purring pussies with a grin on your face as wide as a slice of melon; nor some mean and moody moggie, all slit eyes, taut tail and a coat like barbed-wire bristles.

It doesn't hurt to play the pussy-cat game if you know what you're doing. I reckon to pile up enough good pussy points, all love and affection, so that I can go wild from time to time. Then Mrs Two-Legs will say: 'He's got the wind in his tail' as I go all kamikaze up the curtains, knocking off a vase or two from the window ledge or, tiger-like, rip into the sofa just because it's there!

Scratching is a bit tricky

Scratching, I have to say, is something different, and a bit tricky. As I said, Mrs Two-Legs doesn't like me scratching. I'm not too bothered. I can lie in the garden, yawn a bit, snooze a bit, lick-wash a bit, scratch a bit, plan ahead a bit and lie in the shade of the sun. I don't always plan when I'm going to have a scratching session. Sometimes I just feel the urge or the itch and I scratch. I prefer to use one of my back legs because I get better traction and a faster movement. Obviously, you can't scratch your left side with your right paw and vice versa. If I suddenly get an itch while lying on the sofa, say, on my left side then I have to roll quickly on to my right side so my left hind paw can crack into action. However, if Mrs Two-Legs is present I might defer scratching. In that case, I uncurl from the sofa and walk into the garden and stop behind the shed. That's one of my favourite scratching places, either behind the shed or on its roof where I can stretch out in the sun and have an uninterrupted scratch, my hind leg flashing fast and furious, like a piston. I don't think it's fleas, or if it is it's

I'm dangling there with my dignity all undone

not many. But there are worse things in life than providing a cosy home for a flea. Mrs Two-Legs would go potty, of course.

'He's got fleas again,' she says to the mister, all het up. 'I'm sure of it. He keeps scratching, scratching, scratching. You must dust him again.'

This refers to some white powder which they sprinkle all over me. It goes in my eyes, on my whiskers, sticks to my tail and gets on my paws. It is an affront. They grab me by the scruff of the neck and even though I wriggle, squirm and yelp, I seldom manage to escape. For a cat of my standing in the community, it is highly undignified to be held dangling in the air by Mr Two-Legs out in the garden on their beloved patio, which is nicer than all the neighbours' patios, so they say, while Mrs Two-Legs dollops dust all over me, banging on the bottom of the tub to shoot it out like she was trying to bang tomato sauce out of a bottle.

She says: 'There, there, Louis, we won't hurt you. It's alright.' But it's not alright! I'm dangling there with my dignity all undone.

Next evening I told Minnie about this when she came round to our garden right at the time she had promised and we both climbed up into the laurel. She was disgusted. We were chatting and I could feel a bit of a cuddle coming on when she asked me a question I've never been asked before.

'Louis,' she says, 'have you ever been in an aeroplane?'

10

Time for a little revenge

Afterwards, after all this dusting malarkey, I scoot off sharpish and, just to get my own back, just to show Two-Legs who's boss, I lie in the middle of the lawn where they can see me and I not only roll about a lot to get rid of that horrible powder, but lie down and scratch, really get the legs going faster than a hundred–metre dash. I then stand up on three legs and scratch with the remaining back leg. Afterwards, I ignore them; turn my bare-bottom back on them. If it's a pleasant evening I'll stroll around my patch or perhaps I'll squeeze through the cat flap of one of my chums and grab a bite of cat meat before their mister or missus chases me out all in a dither as if I were going to steal all the sausages in the house! I'll like as not go back late, hiding in the garden under a bush. Then Mrs Two-Legs will come looking for me, whinging into the garden, full of guilt.

'I knew we shouldn't have dusted him,' she whines. Then Mr Two-Legs comes out behind her and says that the dusting was all her idea.

'Well,' she says, 'if you had any love for me or Louis you'd have stopped me. It's all your fault!'

At this point he sighs at the hopelessness of her logic and goes back inside into the front room to watch the telly. He's potty about the news at ten o'clock and keeping up-to-date. When he's talking to a neighbour or a friend who has come visiting and they're sitting in the kitchen having a cup of tea, he might say: 'Did you see the news last night about the Middle East situation?' I am not against the media, although it has to be said there's not a lot on the telly for cats. Nothing about mice or how to best keep your fur looking shiny – not that one is vain, naturally.

Love and devotion for Louis

My mum said that her grandfather – or it might have been her cousin's grandfather – used to like watching BBC TV in the old days before I was born because every so often in the interval they would show fish swimming in a bowl. Grandfather said it was very instructive and got his juices going. So, while old trouser-legs goes off to watch the telly, skirty woman is in the garden all love and devotion for her beloved Louis whom she wouldn't hurt a whisker of for all the cream in Cornwall – unless she thinks he's got fleas and needs sanitising by the scruff of the neck with lots of deadly powder! It is all a question of hygiene – and dead fleas, of course. I mean, where do you draw the line? Certainly, you will find the occasional scruffy moggy, hard pressed to look after himself, low in felicity, low in feline self-esteem without which you can't operate properly.

Anyway, then Mrs Two-Legs comes into the garden looking for me. 'Louis, Louis, Louis,' she shouts. It is not so much shouting as crooning. Sometimes she spreads my name into three parts and dwells on each, going up and down the register, making the second syllable the highest and then descending. Very soppy! Very soppy and a bit humiliating, as if I had not been humiliated enough what with being dangled over the patio by the scruff of the neck and squirted all over with flea powder. It is time for a little revenge. So I mew pitifully, as if my legs were being chewed by one of those long crocodiles you see on the telly, or I'm being dragged backwards tail first through a hedge. I make sure she can't see me so that she goes skittering about the garden – it's dark now – this way and that searching for me. She looks in the bushes, behind the pots on the patio, which is one of my favourite sun-bathing or snoozing spots, and under the trees, particularly the laurel, which I like to climb so that I can see what's going on next door; and she pokes about behind the shed, jabbing here and there with the long canes Mr Two-Legs once used for growing runner beans. After ten minutes or so, she goes bananas. I am following on her heels, but a few feet behind and I'm careful to keep to the shadows where the white of the coat on my chest won't show. I'm mewing all the while. Quite tiring really. At last she runs into the house to get him in long trousers to join the search.

I give myself time to smile a little

'Darling, darling, you must come quick. It's Louis! It's Louis! He must be hurt or something or stuck up a tree. We might have to call the fire brigade.'

I stop mewing to give myself time to smile a little. It's satisfying to see them run around on my behalf. Then Mr Two-Legs comes out. He usually goes to his office in a grey suit or a blue one and carries a briefcase maroon in colour which looks like a suitcase that's shrunk. When he comes home in the evening at 18.40, almost on the dot, he changes his clothes, carefully hanging his suit up. Now he is wearing what he calls his suburban weekend relaxing clothes – jeans and a check shirt, rather a horrible check shirt, actually, all yellows and purples, but then he has no taste and is under some compulsion to go to extremes. It's as if he feels in some strange way that going to extremes not only makes him more masculine but more free. In other words, he's a bit of a plonker!

So when he comes out on to their beloved patio, all seething with rage at being dragged away from the news on the telly by the cat – heavens above! – and worried that he's missed some titbit that one of his colleagues might refer to; and he'll feel foolish and inadequate not only because he doesn't know what they are referring to but because he doesn't know either – which is worse – whether he ought to know and will therefore be tongue-tied, frightened to risk a question, terrified that someone will find him out... So, when he comes out I emerge and wrap myself around his ankles and purr a bit. Generally, this exasperates him totally and he opens a bottle. He shouts at her and she snaps back but when he has stomped back into the house she comes over and 'diddums' me, crooning: 'There's a good diddums-do. There's a lovely puss. Who nearly got lost then? Poor pussy.'

I allow her to tickle me

I sit on my hind legs with my forelegs straight in front in the Egyptian posture and turn my head a little as I allow her to tickle me under one ear. I sit in the middle of the patio because when the kitchen curtains are not closed the light from the kitchen floods the patio and, as I see on the telly, it's a bit like sitting in the spotlight on the pitch at Wembley where lots of Two-Legs in short trousers run around kicking a ball.

So hygiene is an early problem for our parliament. We need to say what is reasonable for Two-Legs to inflict on their feline companions, and what not. We need to start from the premise that the feline fraternity is inherently cleaner than Two-Legs. Cats are always washing themselves, whether indoors or out. How many Two-Legs do you see having a wash outside their homes? I hear that on the underground tube a woman will sometimes 'put her face on,' as they say, to apply lipstick to her lips, powder to her cheeks, mascara to her eyelashes, eye shadow to her eyes and a dab of scent here and there, to wrists, neck and behind the ears. But you don't see them having a wash in the tube. There's no stripping off and splashing about with water and flannels and soap and towels and having a good rub down. You seldom see it in the street either. If I take a saunter along Barnet (West) high street, high on the hill, just to check what's going on, I don't expect to see a man pouring a bucket of water over his head or a woman sitting in a tin bath by the traffic lights scrubbing her back with a loofah.

All this washing business has moved indoors and generally behind closed doors. It is a big paraphernalia with a lot of lotions and potions, not so much to make you clean as to make you smell nice, keep your skin soft, or make your hair shine. They have different soap for their hair. It is a wonder there is not face soap, arm soap, tummy soap, leg soap, knee soap, armpit soap, big-toe soap, going to work soap, coming home soap or soap for very rare occasions such as voting, which we should have to call democratic soap. All this soap cuts no ice with cats. We don't use it, don't need it. We have a rough and ever-ready tongue. Whoever saw a cat with a flannel? Or a toothbrush? Or some lotion or potion specially felinised to shampoo my coat and make it shiny, glossy and gleaming with extra vitamin E, evening primrose oil and essence of kipper?

Minnie's coat is gleaming. She looks a very well cat, whiskers very proportionate, very dainty paws, all white as snow, of course. And you can see from her face that she smiles a lot. But she was frowning when she asked that question about aeroplanes. I didn't want to lower her impression of me as a knowledgeable leader of the feline community and admit I'd never been in an aeroplane so I turned the tables a bit. I said: 'Why do you ask?'

I don't expect to see this
at the traffic lights

46

11

A state of poise

Cats are inherently clean and hygienic, even if we have to go to the loo in the garden. Humans have stopped doing that – in the London Borough of Barnet (West) anyway – which is a pity. There is something very civilised about letting nature take its course in the open air. Not only does it expose all your covered-up parts to the environment – never mind if it is raining – but it is also an opportunity to stop for a moment and look around.

Part of our parliamentary proceedings will be devoted to human-feline relations: we shall have a committee. A sub-committee of that committee will concern education for Two-Legs, part of its remit being getting them to stop. They do rush about; their bodies rush about and their heads rush about. When that is not enough, they get into cars or aeroplanes and rush about some more. Cats know that here is the same as there only different, but the humans always seem to be looking for something extra to what they already have. We would hope to teach them to do nothing for a couple of hours a day. This is what you might call elementary hygiene for the mind. Unless someone is chasing me, or I'm chasing a bird or a squirrel, I am in a state of poise. That is to say, a state of equilibrium: not too hot, not too cold, not too full, not too empty, not too cheerful, not too sad, not too optimistic, not too pessimistic, not too much wishing I was in the garden, not too much wishing I was in the kitchen, not too much wishing to be even more handsome, not too much just a little less, not too much wishing my whiskers were longer and more wavy, not too much that they were straighter and shorter. You need poise.

I can climb higher up trees

Sometimes I sit for a long time, just doing nothing, filling up my tank. When the tank's full, you know it. When my tank's full I can climb higher up trees. But I am content to sit and do nothing.

My mister and missus have two lots of curtains in the room they call the front room, one behind the other and I can squiggle behind them both and sit in the corner on my back legs in the Egyptian stance and look out of the window. A road goes by outside and I can see the cars pass and the people pass and the children go off in a rush, all clean and tidy for school in the morning, and come home all of a dawdle in the afternoon, messy and untidy, often eating, sometimes the girls arm-in-arm, chatting.

One lot of curtains is made of net, a white net with flower patterns on it, and sometimes it drapes over my back as I've pushed underneath it. I don't mind – though generally I can't abide any sort of clothes, except when the children – the mister and missus's children – were little and used to dress me up in pyjamas. The white net is a sort of cape and I imagine it looks quite flattering against the shiny black of my fur. Sometimes as they pass, the Two-Legs say: 'Look at that handsome cat in the window,' and point me out to their children. At least that's what I expect they say.

'Look at that handsome cat in the window'

Sitting, just sitting, is good for you. I do it a lot. Mind you, I don't have to earn a living. If necessary, I could feed myself and find somewhere to sleep but the Two-Legs are looking after me. I'm grateful in my own way, and I show it sometimes in my own way. For example, I might go up to their bedroom early one morning and pad about on their bed until they wake up or else find a comfortable hollow to nestle into. They don't always appreciate waking up early but I have learned to accept their ingratitude. I'm a very cool cat so I'm not bothered. They don't really mean to express their negative emotions, even when I'm snuggled down beside the big mister. On one occasion he must have thought I was Mrs Two-Legs, or at least her hair, for when he was still somewhat asleep, he gave me a big huggy kiss and then woke up with a start. 'Damn cat,' he shouts. 'What is it, George?' she says, all solicitous. She discovers it's me and comes over all diddums-do and poor pussy but not too much so as to upset her George. He is quick to take umbrage.

As a cat one has a natural sense to know what behaviour is appropriate. However, the mister seems to lose his sense of what's appropriate from time to time. He's all smiles and politeness when he and Betty are entertaining the Robinsons or the Gilberts and the new Mrs Gilbert of the frizzy hair and cold-in-her-nose spills soup over me just because I jump on her lap, all friendly like, and Mr Two-Legs says not to worry with a smile, it was an old table cloth anyway and the carpet won't stain anyway, he's all smiles then. However, when I land on their bed and pad up and down on the duvet, occasionally testing my claws on the duvet cover, or if I lick his ear if it's not covered by the bed clothes, partly as a gesture of respect and partly out of curiosity to see if the sandpaper roughness of my tongue is sufficiently strong to penetrate his sleep state and wake him up – then he doesn't seem all smiles in adversity at all. Instead, he leaps up, wide awake, shouting: 'That damn cat!'

I suspect he works too hard and does all the wrong things. Certainly you don't see him sitting in the Egyptian posture much, or what would correspond to that posture if Two-Legs had back legs, which they don't. It is remarkable that they can walk on two legs. I try it sometimes when no one is looking but it is not only difficult but also tiring and it's hard to know what to do with one's paws. The humans swing their paws when they walk. When I walk on two legs I hold my paws out in front as if I'm playing the piano but I feel silly and don't do it for long. Perhaps Two-Legs like swinging their arms; perhaps they are under an obligation to swing them for so many times a day for reasons of health; or perhaps it is a condition for living in Barnet (West) high on the hill. Perhaps you have to swing your arms like a soldier so many times a day or they won't collect your rubbish from your dustbins every week.

When I wash, I tend to do many repetitions on one paw and then the other, depending on what day of the week it is. Our mum said we had to be cleaner every day as the week went on so that we could be really clean on Sundays. She said that Sunday is a special day of rest.

When I walk on two legs I hold my paws out in front

So I tend to follow my mum's advice and wash a little harder as the days go by. Cats, as we've said, are inherently hygienic. This is a point that we need to get across to Two-Legs to ensure reciprocal hygienic respect; and which we must address in our parliament. We are not asking for a portable loo by a cabbage patch in the garden nor that old Two-Legs should forsake their tiled bathrooms, all very nice and warm, for a cold draught on a bare bottom under an apple tree. But by the use of feline plea power – and this must be high on the agenda for early discussion in our Bill of Rights – we shall denounce the use of feline flea powder.

Minnie tearful

I'm sure that Minnie would agree to that. I'm getting to quite like her and also I'm feeling a bit sad because of her problem. She lives at the other end of the street with Mr Fraser (Minnie says he's a bit of a clown) and his wife Sarah and their two children, Isaac and Ruby. She's very happy there, she says, and Ruby couldn't do more for her, very loving and affectionate. But when she was telling me this as we snuggled close together for warmth in the fork of the laurel tree, little Minnie – it touches me she's so small – little Minnie started to get a bit tearful on account of her problem. Although I was anxious to know what it was and to help her, I suggested she should stop now, particularly as it was getting dark. So we climbed down and I walked her home.

Are your whiskers straight, curly, or droopy?

12

College for cats

We may need some training in political representation and parliamentary affairs, although it has to be said that the politicians in Westminster seem to get by without it – or perhaps they don't. If there were a school for politicians they would all sound the same, even more than they do now. The training we require is really for those cats with little metropolitan experience. While it is true that all cats have a high IQ, some higher than others, of course, not all have been exposed to the sophistication that inevitably arises from mingling in the metropolis with the cognoscenti of cats, such as is my daily round, albeit not every day, naturally. A reflective cat needs time for meditation, for peace and quiet.

Training would be useful in the matter of debate – perhaps we need to open a college for the sophistication of cats where such matters could be dealt with. We would not call it a school for sophistication but rather a cats' academy for cultural instruction where we could study a variety of moggy modules. We might concern ourselves, for example, with a study of the interaction between the air and bodies, that is cats flying through the air, as when we have to leap from roof to roof.

Some of the brighter cats, those who after all will be our leaders in the future, the setters of fashion, will help formulate our new constitution – and a new constitution must be of paramount importance. A constitution would cover some of the subjects we have already touched on, such as inter-personal relations feline–human–wise; the theory, function and variety of the miaow; live or tinned food; rights of abode including reasonable wear and tear of carpets, curtains and claws, the latter subject of claws to be more fully covered in the subject of cosmetics for cats; minimum standards of floor coverings for cats, or what you might call paw laws; the acceptable limits of caterwauling at night; and of course, whiskers.

The study of whiskers

A most important subject is the study of whiskers, their care, deportment, the variety of styles and the interpretation of the feline psyche according to the manner in which a cat's whiskers address the world, that is to say, the nuance of angle, pitch and plane, the attitude of assertion or denial as well as the inherent quality of straightness, curliness or droop, not to mention the length of whisker which, some whiskerologists suggest, is indicative of how many times a cat has lived before; or, given that a cat has nine lives, how many are left.

Although I am a tolerant cat without a narrow mind who likes to take a broad view, I think such ideas are rubbish. However, this is not the time or place to enter into the great debate on the fundamental meaning of whiskers. Anyway, the whiskerologists tend to forget that a cat has not just one whisker or one pair of whiskers but a bunch of whiskers. Symmetry is the word here, equal number of whiskers, neatly paired on either side of the face and, ideally, of equal poise and precision and, preferably, what you might call an harmonic of length, or a rainbow of size. That means they are not necessarily all the same length but, depending where you start, get longer or shorter in a graduated curve that is both graceful and pleasing.

Whiskers can also be studied, interpreted and codified according to colour and what you might call timbre, that is the essence of whisker or ultimate 'whiskerality'. While I concede that it may be necessary, and indeed it is necessary, that somewhere on the planet, as we rush through space and rush through our lives, that some high-powered academic puss pores over the statistics, logistics and what you might call the gymnastics of whiskers, that is to say, the suppleness of their curl and twirl, their quirks and perks, it is important to be mindful that there is more to feline consciousness than concern over their whiskers. We have our part to play in the evolutionary development of the planet and a first stop has to be our own parliament and the full representation of all British moggies.

What qualifications, if any, would be required before a feline could vote is a matter to be decided. It is hoped that the proclamation of these few, poor humble words might lead to the formation of a committee to look into the possibility of a Parliament for Cats. Such a committee would obviously include some of the old grey and grizzled cats as well as the young strutters who think they can leap any wall, climb any tree, cross any

She looked away but there was nothing to see

roof. Not that any of the young cats of today could match what we got up to when I was young, of course, but they could probably try. Nowadays their claws don't seem quite so sharp, nor their tails so snappy.

To snap your tail is similar but not the same as cracking a whip. In my day, we would compete with each other for the snappiest tail. I can still hear my old mum saying: 'Don't you go snapping your tail with all those other silly cats. When you grow up you'll realise what a good friend your tail is to you. Now, you don't want to injure it with "snap, snap, snap".'

She was right, of course, but all of us kittens couldn't help but notice that she snapped her tail to emphasise the words 'snap, snap, snap'. And what a good tail-snapper was she! When I was grown up and visiting her one day when her eyes weren't too good and she was getting so she could hardly tell a mouse from the moon, I said to her where did she learn to snap her tail like that? At once, her paw shot out and she cuffed my ear.

'You treat your mother with respect,' she said.

Later, when we'd eaten, and some of my brothers and sisters had arrived – we were a big family – she started talking about her young days. My sister Molly, who was a bit of a favourite of mum, although I didn't think she was particularly special just because she had a patch of ginger on her black-and-white coat, Molly said to mum were there any good, really good tail-snappers in her day? Mum's face took on a far-away smile and her whiskers quivered a little and then relaxed.

'As a matter of fact,' she said, 'there were.'

She looked into the distance. We were clustered in a

favourite spot beneath the laurel tree and near the hedge at the bottom of the garden where no one could see us. She looked away but there was nothing to see except the dark green leaves of the hedge and I don't think she saw that. In her mind she was seeing scenes from her youth when she was more springy and leapy than now. She was getting old.

'One of the girls was a very fast snapper,' she said. 'Her name was – .' She paused while she hunted in her mind for a name. 'Victoria,' she announced, pleased with herself for finding the name. And I couldn't tell whether it was real or made up for the occasion.

'We would call her Vicky – only when she was a grandma, many kittens later, did we call her Victoria. Vicky was a very fast tail-snapper: fast, sharp and lethal. You didn't get in the way of her tail. Oh no! None of the boys could touch her for speed. She was a good climber and leaper, too. But best of all, she was so pretty.'

She was still a handsome cat

When she said that her face took on such a smile of warmth, a sort of smile that sank right into her, and a look of pride that reached right round to her eyes. We knew that in the only way her modesty would allow that she was talking about herself – and even in her old age she was still a handsome cat. She still made many a whisker twitch. When she died, they buried her near the sundial on the lawn. The children were young then and cried and Mrs Two-Legs was not dry-eyed. Mum used to like sitting near that sundial in the sunshine. Many a time I remember playing by it and mum chasing me round and round.

So we shall need youth and maturity for our parliament, energy and wisdom. My mum would have been good at the wisdom bit. Minnie would be wise and youthful and a great asset to our parliament. She is kind and beautiful – a great example to younger cats. And she's got a good head on her shoulders. There's only one problem. At last she explained it to me when she came round one evening. She had been sitting waiting for me. I was a little late – parliamentary matters detained me. I came along and without a word, just a look, we both climbed up to our favourite nook in the laurel tree. It's almost a seat where two thick branches come together. I thought she was going to fall out of the tree as she started quivering and shaking almost unable to tell me her problem. Then out it came. She was going to be leaving Barnet (West) high on the hill. I couldn't believe it. I almost fell out of the tree – and it was such bad news that if I didn't fall, I almost wanted to.

We climbed up into our favourite tree

61

13

Understanding the miaow

An early task for our Parliament for Cats is to set up a commission, perhaps even a permanent commission, to study and advise on the complex problem of British cat language. There is more to cat language than a miaow. This miaow is not to be despised nor denigrated or in any way minimised. For, as almost every feline knows, the miaow is fundamental. Every cat has one, although it has to be said, the way it is used varies enormously. It can be long or short, squeaky or melodious, more of a rattle or more of a drum, poignant or purry, song-like or saucy.

Generally speaking, it is the only cat-sound the humans hear. We have the task of making known all our needs and wants through this two-syllable utterance and we have to find ways of manipulating its sound to express their variety. It is not very easy.

Most Two-Legs assume that we make a miaow just to get their attention. If I sit by my bowl and make the miaow, they will assume I want to be fed. I do want to be fed, of course, and that is why I am making this miaow but it is an example of the tall people's lack of understanding that I'm forced to communicate in this coarse and rudimentary fashion. Given the choice, I would say: 'Thank you mister and missus tall persons for all the food to date. You are most kind and generous and you will always have good karma cat-wise. May I presume to say, I rather fancy some breast of chicken for supper tonight followed by a few spoonfuls of cream? Maybe later, if you are going to watch television, I'll come and sit on your lap and purr a bit. I could do with some shut-eye before I go out later because it looks like being a heavy night. My friends have given me the nod.'

The music of the miaow

Instead of that, I just have to sit by my bowl and make the miaow. However, long experience and numerous experiments have shown that the tall chaps and chapesses are incapable of tuning in to the refinements of the miaow, of discerning its inherent music, and the meaning of this moggy mew. By pitch and intonation, timbre and hue, this one small voice can suggest as many meanings as there are leaves on a laurel.

For example, if I wanted to express my delight that Mrs Two-Legs was making pork pies and there was a good chance that a crumb or two might come my way, then the miaow would have three 'curves' in it, so to speak, that is, the 'wow!' part repeated three times in a wave-like or crescendo form.

How can we get Two-Legs to understand the miaow?

If I wished to observe that the cushions on the sofa are not so plump as they used to be, now that I'm not so young as I used to be, then I'd put more of a 'yowl' into the miaow, not a howl, please note, which would be inappropriate behaviour, but a 'yowl', which is like flexing your jaw from side to side as you maintain pressure in the belly. It is important that the miaow is not mistaken for a growl, which is more used in situations of hostility, or perplexity – as when a wall goes 'live' for a moment and you sit there entranced.

How can we get the tall people to understand the miaow and its subtle variations? Truly, we could publish a dictionary of the miaow and its interpretations. However, since there is but little variation between British cat-speak and moggy lingo the world over – although the style of expression may range from the tigerish to the timorous – a study of the miaow would be of great benefit in the quest for international understanding. If the miaow can be interpreted in the same way in Timbuktu or Texas, Bombay or Barnet then in the shape of the humble moggy's miaow we have a priceless instrument for international communication. Such is the power of the feline voice.

That, of course, is the vision, the great vision for humanity from the feline perspective. It makes me purr to even think about it.

The tall people have always assumed that our purring is a sign of content or pleasure. Indeed it is. But, like the moggy's miaow, which is an offering to Two-Legs, an example and a demonstration of how things might be, so is the cat's purr. It is at once a sign of ease and content and also a continuously offered lesson. The lesson is – take it easy chaps and chapesses. Your pursuit of this and that is a bit over the top. Better stop, take a couple of days off and purr a bit. What is the most purr-making thing I know? That is a good question to ask yourself. Tum-tickling makes me purr – not that I'd want that all day – but Two-Legs needs not so much pleasure – the pursuit of which can be much less than pleasurable – as a bit of ease. Certainly, our timetable in the Parliament for Cats would allow time for tum-tickling.

Scheduled tum-tickling time

Should the leader of the house stand up and demand what the member for Barnet (West) meant by such and such a remark and the said member for Barnet (West) could not be found, it would be perfectly acceptable for the speaker to say: 'I have to advise the leader of the house that the member for Barnet (West) is on his scheduled tum-tickling time.' The speaker might then say: 'Let us all adjourn for ten minutes tum-tickling.'

In my thoughts for the future and our Parliament for Cats I realised I was including little Minnie. I said to myself why is this old rogue of a bachelor cat getting all soppy over a little white cat called Minnie, so tiny and so furry and so, well, lovable?

I thought of a basket for two. Would Mrs Two-Legs (never mind Mr Two-Legs, in affairs of the heart, he doesn't count) would Mrs Two-Legs let Minnie through the cat flap and stay with me? Then I remembered: she was leaving the London Borough of Barnet (West) high on the hill. It made me feel sick.

14

What should we wear in our Parliament?

We need to consider what we should wear in our Parliament for Cats. Normally, we wear nothing at all unless one of the tall ones is sufficiently lacking in respect and appreciation of our dignity to fix a collar round our necks, sometimes with a bell attached. This is not only undignified but irritating. It is also an affront to one's self-esteem if the collar is a ghastly red or blue. These are colours which jar horribly with the colour of one's coat and can cause a refined feline to wince with shame. The tall ones do not always understand why this should be so, but they only have to put a collar round their own neck to see how it feels. Imagine them walking up the high street in Barnet (West) high on the hill with a red leather collar, bell attached. The only good thing might be that the bell tinkled as they talked and cut down the gossip as they loitered in the supermarket, trolley to trolley.

But what should we wear in our Parliament? The tall people wear many uniforms according to their jobs, or who they mix with, or who they think they are. It all seems very odd. I can't imagine changing my black-and-white coat just because I'm going out for a stroll or a roof-top ramble with Geronimo the ginger tom from the house at 43, or putting on a striped waistcoat and short trousers so as not to offend the onlookers' sensibilities when climbing trees with Tiger Tim, the tabby from 109. And on those evenings or midnights when we congregate by some Barnet (West) back-garden shed should we all – Geronimo the ginger tom, Tiger Tim the tabby, Eustace the Persian, Terence the tortoiseshell, Hermione and Lilly the lilac twins – should we all dress in blue jeans to demonstrate our unity or our accord – or, it has to be said – our common folly?

Can you see us all sitting there on the roof in bright blue jeans? But this is what the two-legged brigade do. Our postman has a blue uniform, though it's rather dark, and our insurance man who calls once a month has a different sort of uniform: it's not so much a uniform of matching jacket and trousers as a similar style. When Henrietta, our friendly Havana, when Henrietta's folks had a wedding – it was for their daughter Jane who is tall and thin like a lamppost without the lamp – when they had a wedding everyone put on a uniform for the day. Jane, the bride, was in white, the bridegroom Timothy and all the other men wore black with long coats with two tails at the back, which looked a bit ridiculous since they weren't tails you could do anything with: you couldn't flick them, or snap them like a whip, or curl them over your ear. And why two tails? It seems most unnatural! Little girls who were bridesmaids wore pink. After the ceremony everyone had a meal and a dance and then the bride and groom changed their clothes and left half way through the dancing. Everyone went on dancing as if they were pleased the couple had gone.

My friend Max, who is black all over and lives at 22 with a white mischief-maker called Sylvia who thinks she's a bit special because she got locked in her folks' loft for two days when her mister and missus were on holiday, my friend Max, who says he's probably the most black cat of all the cats in the London Borough of Barnet (West), our Max said that when the firemen came to get Sylvia out of the loft they all had firemen's uniforms on with big boots, big helmets and axes. The question is: do we

We could put wigs on our heads like barristers and judges

want to dress up in a lot of clobber for our Parliament for Cats?

There are all sorts of uniforms we could choose. We could put wigs on our heads like barristers and judges or we could all wear ball gowns with hooped petticoats. We could dress like schoolboys with short grey trousers, a blazer and a cap, or like a trapeze artist in a leopard-skin leotard. Some might prefer the football boots and shirts of some famous team like Arsenal or the bowler hat and brolly of some smooth-suited city gent. It's all a question of taste. We could change our apparel one month so that we looked like spacemen, and the next like doctors and nurses or bishops and popes or cowboys and soldiers. What should we wear in our Parliament?

Robes trimmed with ermine

Will nothing at all be good enough? Or should we wear something trivial just to make a point? I'm not suggesting robes trimmed with ermine, which would be an insult to stoats, but perhaps fluffy cuffs and lacy trim around the ankles. Perhaps we might develop the sort of bib that sailors wear. It could be squarish and white with a border or borders of blue, the number of borders to denote seniority. After all, one needs a little recognition for one's unselfish and unswerving devotion to duty. Not that one would wish to emulate the honours system among the upper-class Two-Legs with all those lords and ladies and knights and whatnot. My friend Posy (Posy-Rosy we call her on account of what might almost be a dash of pink in her ginger coat) Posy, who's at 44, has some good ideas at times but her suggestion that we should have rings around our tails is not one of her best. When wishing to attract the speaker's attention, we should have our tails in the upright position. What with the rings and everything else, that all sounds a little too like a hoopla stall.

If Buckingham Palace wrote saying would I accept a knighthood I would probably refuse. I'm not so sure that Sir Louis would suit me. On the other hand if they wanted to make me a lord I should have to think more carefully. One has to consider that if such an honour is offered, it must have been earned. Moreover, there is one's family and friends to think of. Would a refusal disappoint them? There is also a certain ring to Lord Louis of Birchwood, London Borough of Barnet (West), high on the hill.

What should we wear in our Parliament for Cats? Certainly boots, shoes or sandals. Myself, I would prefer black, high-stepping boots for the back paws and white gloves or slippers for the front paws. You have to bear in mind that when old Two-Legs goes indoors he takes his shoes off – at least some of them do. We, on the other hand, go barefoot – or bare-pawed – all the time. When we enter our debating chamber we would not want to carry in the dirt and dust from our paws and so it is boots, shoes or sandals – or paw-washing. However, we are not very keen on getting our paws wet. You never know when you might have to race up a tree. Keep your claws dry, my mum always said.

We would probably not want to wear hats. Not only

would we have to debate endlessly whether members would have a free choice on what headgear to wear, but if we opted to wear hats we should have to decide not only on bonnet, bowler, cap or crown but also, since we have ears that are perky and alert – unlike those floppy dogs who have a bend in their ears, like a flap on an envelope – we should need to agree whether the ears should be worn through the bonnet, bowler, cap, or crown thus needing to cut holes for our ears, or contained within the bonnet, bowler, cap or crown, thus requiring an enlargement of the same. We might say that what members wore or did not wear was their affair and many would rejoice in appearing unclad, as naked as nature intended.

However, we would need decisions on tails and the precise etiquette for determining their deportment. Obviously, such regulations would only apply to those cats with tails. Those without, or those whose tails are below a certain length, would be excepted but that would in no way marginalise them.

She put one paw over my shoulder. I didn't say anything but I was very pleased

Indeed, it is to be hoped that, on all sides of the house, a definite proportion – not too large, one would add – would be tail-less or tail-challenged. Some of my best friends are tail-challenged; short of tail, perhaps, but not short of verve or vivacity.

She never knew her mum

Certainly Minnie would know what to wear in parliament. But am I just fooling myself in dreaming a dream that is just not going to happen? I wanted to take her to Lavender Isle. She tells me she's never been. Apparently, her mother never showed her the way. But then, like a lot of cats, she hardly knew her mum. She was given away almost before she could walk. So I told her a bit about Lavender Isle and how we would get there. She was very excited. She put one paw over my shoulder. I didn't say anything but I was very pleased. It prompted me to pass on a special secret word my mum gave me for ease in times of difficulty or for gratitude in times of joy. I asked mum if the word had been passed down since ancient times, remembering when in Egypt we had been favoured by the pharaohs – not exactly royal cats, but something like that. My mum wouldn't say it was but she wouldn't say it wasn't. There was a smile to her face and a mystery and her tail moved slowly. But as I was thinking of telling my little Minnie about the secret word, a bird flew by: we both turned our heads and the moment passed. Perhaps I'll tell her later.

Such a moggy is like a deadly missile ready for launching

15

What shall we do about dogs?

We would have to do something about dogs. We do admit they exist, of course, and that there is some fraternisation between them and us. One would not wish to condemn them out of hand – but the grown, wise and mature cat, which is – one has to say – the majority of my fellow felines, will not condone any canine collaboration. For every snarl, a hiss; for every bark, a yeowl; for every scintilla of affection, extreme distaste. One might have to arch one's back, extend one's claws and growl. Regrettably, those canny canines have secured the field in growling. Their growling, however, is nothing but a tummy rumble compared to the deep-throat ferocity of a snarling feline. That ferocity is daunting. Indeed, it is lethal. A cat hunched-up, low on the ground, snarling, fur standing fierce like spikes on a brush, face with anger drawn and contorted, teeth flared for combat, such a moggy is like a deadly missile ready for launching. Not that in our Parliament for Cats would we have any snarling, spitting, scratching or clawing of the sort that would bring feline felicity into disrepute. Members would be required not to unsheathe their claws, nor writhe their tails in anger. The slight jerk or twist of a tail in order for a member to make himself or herself comfortable would not be unacceptable and we would probably need to have some sort of regulations regarding tail-curve in body-hugging mode. While it is natural and proper for cats to curl their tails around themselves – a source of comfort for some perhaps – our dear mother always said: 'A neat tail makes for a neat moggy.' So we were taught to use the tail wisely, to curl it around the body when lying down or around the front paws when sitting on the back legs in order to look tidy and all-of-a-piece. Moreover, old Two-Legs with his boots and shoes is less likely to tread on one's tail if it's not stretched out straight like a broomstick. Tail

**When I curl up like this,
I can wrap my tail round me**

76

deportment or tail management is one of the first things an intelligent mother teaches her kittens.

When a sleeping moggie curls up like a ball, chin on toes, the tail can wrap around the body in the same way that Two-Legs lays a long thin cushion at the foot of the door to keep out the draughts. The tip of the tail can cover the eyes, which can be useful if the sun is shining directly – or one feels like hiding. For instance, I was lying on the window ledge, a surface which is a little bit harder than I'm used to, enjoying the heat from the radiator below and the sunshine through the window, eyes covered with the tip of my tail, dozing a bit and musing on old times when I was a frisky fellow, when in comes Mrs Two-Legs, all bossy, like she often is.

'What are you up to, Louis?' she says, with a duster in one hand. It's perfectly obvious that I'm having a bit of a snooze but here she is questioning me like a music-hall policeman. 'I say, I say, I say, what 's going on 'ere then?'

Expose one's tum

On such occasions, by moving the tip of my tail just a smidgen, I can watch her every move and pretend to be asleep. Sometimes she will leave the room and sometimes she will come and stroke me or even tickle me under the chin. One doesn't necessarily mind that too much; indeed the tactile sensations can be quite pleasant. One has even been known to roll over on one's back and expose one's tum. However, the window ledge above the radiator is narrow and one could lose

If she got on with her dusting instead of tickling my chin...

one's dignity by falling off. Indeed, one nearly did fall off one morning and there was much scrabbling about.

'Mind yourself, Louis,' says Mrs Two-Legs.

If she got on with her dusting instead of tickling my chin, these things wouldn't happen and a gentlemanly cat of the older generation wouldn't be scrabbling about, whiskers all of a twitch, trying not to do a backward somersault off the ledge all on account of her tickling fingers. And, anyway, she might provide a cushion for me to lie on. She knows I like to be there. She knows it's a favourite spot.

'Are you sitting watching the world go by, Louis?' she says – tickle, tickle, tickle. She says some daft things and for some reason when she is being affectionate, she changes her voice so that it's high-pitched and cooing. I tolerate this because I have a lot of sympathy for the tall Two-Legs lot. They have a hard time and a busy time. They don't seem to sit on window ledges like me and watch the world tick by a little.

Mrs Tall Two-Legs would say: 'I've got housework and shopping and the Robinsons and the Gilberts are coming for dinner tonight. And she's such a good cook!'

When you just watch, you see what goes by. You can wash your paws or shine up your coat and just watch a little. You can close your eyes or open them and if I see a blackbird or a sparrow fly by then I might breathe a little faster and tense my tail but I'm not too bothered. There's time to take your time.

Barnabus, the barber-shop cat in the London Borough of Barnet (West) high street, high on the hill, sits in the window most of the day. The customers talk to him as they come in and out but Barnabus doesn't pay much attention. There is a skill, of course, in just watching, which Two-Legs don't seem to possess much. Sitting about is not so much being lazy as taking time to gather your energy into a fullness so you can properly watch and take well thought-out decisions, such as when to go out for a quiet stroll over the lawn in the garden or when to turn into a frenzy and rush up and down the stairs a bit and in and out of the rooms as if one's tail were on fire. This frenzy, this rushing about like a jet-propelled tornado, disturbs them. Mrs Two-Legs says to her husband or to herself or just to the heavens: 'Oh dear! What's Louis up to now?'

This time her voice doesn't sound like she's sucking on sugar lumps. It sounds cross, as if she's just fallen over and torn her skirt. I'm glad I don't have to wear a skirt or trousers. Mr Two-Legs wears boxer shorts with stripes. His suits have stripes, his shirts have stripes, and his ties have stripes. The suits are grey and blue, the shirts are pink and white, and the ties are blue and gold. If you count the stripe in his hair, which is where he parts his hair, one side to the left, one side to the right, he is a very stripy person. He has black shoes with polished toe caps like black buns and when he goes off to the office, he looks like a very smart person. All these stripes, however, are either on account of fashion or he has some sort of hidden zebra fascination. He wasn't born with stripes.

Neither of the Two-Legs has tails. That is probably a good thing because they would be endlessly fussing over them – magazine articles on how to make your tail look stunning or whether it's best worn inside your skirt or trousers or outside your skirt or trousers. Doubtless there would be tail shops, false tails, special tail diets and politically-correct tail posture as well as aerobics for tails not to mention tell-tail signs by which to tell your fortune; and probably competitions for the longest, shortest, most beautiful tail, most glamorous tail, most anonymous tail, most unassuming tail, most unlike-a-tail tail.

Tail management

Fortunately, we felines have more sense, although it is right and proper that we give due importance to tail management; and the etiquette – or you might say kitty-quette – of tail behaviour would be an early item on the agenda of our new parliament. We might consider having tail bars behind our seats over which, if we so wished, we could drape our tails. This, if taken up as a custom by members, would not only offer a degree of rest and comfort but also a certain charm or style to the chamber, bearing in mind that in terms of appearance we are multi-coloured, multi-cultural, multi-hued and hairy moggies with tails to boot, although not so stripy as some of our other mammalian colleagues.

So there are many factors concerning dress, deportment and procedure which will need to be discussed – and discussion itself needs to be contained within a structure. It is regrettably true that not all of my fellow felines will have reached that maturity of mind which marks out those of us who may well be on the front bench of our parliament. One does not wish to be arrogant, boastful or proud but it is observable that the mature moggie can sometimes be hard to find. Some are parochially based, territorial in outlook – what I call lamppost cats. Their thinking extends no further than the area they have marked out from this lamppost to that tree, this rose bush in the back garden to the holly. And woe betide any lurking feline who crosses their borders! Much hissing, spitting, yowling and belly-throated growling and even – one is embarrassed to admit – fighting. Still, perhaps it is fair to say that, just like Two-Legs, part of us is still animal!

One has to confess that there are some nights when I let myself out for what you might call a friendly stroll around the parish, saying hallo to a few chums, padding along with tail in upright mode, maintaining the sense of dignity and propriety that befits one's station in life, having regrettably to ignore one or two of my fellow felines whose behaviour and reputation may be discerned by their ragged ears, sawn-off whiskers and a coat which, far from being sleek and smooth, is bald in patches, corrugated and spiky as if they've been run over by a blunt lawnmower. There are other nights,

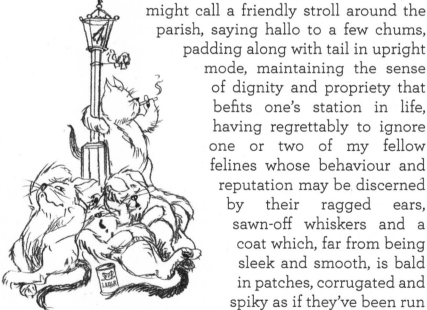

Lamppost cats with ragged ears and sawn-off whiskers

however, when one finds it difficult not to slink from shadow to shadow, avoiding the moonlight, leaping over walls, scooting up fences, and slithering, slipping and sliding from one rooftop to the next.

Sometimes I skedaddle across the lawn, tail up, ears back as if I were being chased by a tiger. I go fast, turning this way and that, fighting off a hundred imaginary predators as I jet, helter-skelter between the daffodils and daisies. When I get puffed, I stop. Sometimes I will stare a bit.

Could I go to Lavender Isle?

As I said, and as I told Minnie when we were sitting all snug in the bosom of the laurel tree one warm summer night – the fact is that when cats sit staring at a wall or a tree or just into space they may be journeying towards the Lavender Isle. She found it hard to believe. She asked a question I hadn't thought of. She said: 'Suppose I'm a long way away in a different country. If I were looking at a wall or a tree as you describe – and once I knew how to travel there, of course – could I go to Lavender Isle?'

'Of course,' I said. 'Of course.'

I was all of a flutter inside wondering where this was leading. She told me as I walked her home. She said Mr Fraser and family were going to a country called New Zealand where his wife Sarah had been offered a new job. She had been born in that country.

It was a long time until I saw Minnie again.

Riding around the universe, checking on the stars

16

A secret shared

There is much to be done before we can establish our Parliament for Cats. Naturally enough, I have spoken – nay canvassed – the cats in the street where I live in the London Borough of Barnet (West), high on the hill. Among others they are Zipper and Pip at 3a; Buddy and Benji , two short-haired black brothers at 15; Kimba and Kingston at 17; Paddington at 21; Custard and Treacle at 25; Kuscha, a short-haired Bengal, fierce and bit stripy at 33; Lenny, the lemonade cat at number 46, a long-haired Persian; and Snowy at 124, who is as white as Minnie but larger and more fluffy; Cheema at 79a; and, of course, Barnabus, the barber-shop cat, a semi-long-haired Balinese. There is some enthusiasm among my fellow felines for our parliament but not yet that bounding passion you feel when Mrs Two-Legs raps your dish with a spoon and shouts: 'Din dins, Louis.'

What we need are some controversial issues to evoke or rouse their interest. For example, the possibility of having tins of cat food provided which can be digitally opened with the touch of a paw or, if you have the strength in your hind parts, a push from the tip of your tail. And, of course, our own fridges which, in the same way, can be opened with a digital paw.

A well-kept secret

However, what really prevents us forging ahead on all four paws is the lack of an important decision which, until now, has been a very well-kept secret, even since ancient times. The truth is that when a cat sits staring at a wall, or just sits in the garden looking into space, you might think that they are doing nothing at all but he, or she, may be far, far away, in their invisible form. There is this island, as I've said, called the Lavender Isle, which we can visit in our unseen form at any time we choose. I wish I could say where it is but if I say it is half-way to here and there and then back again, and a little to the left, and, moreover, it is invisible to those who can only see the visible, you will understand the difficulty of stating a precise geographic location. It is a sweet-smelling island, and not for nothing known as the Lavender Isle. It gladdens your heart. The sages of old times sometimes visit. Lord Buddha has a cottage there next to the old Chinese sage, Lao-tzu. Their cottages are beside the stream which runs in a lazy route through the trees of the forest. Lord Buddha was perturbed to hear stories that the universe was expanding. He knew this wasn't true, of course, since the universe is all there is, which is everything. Nonetheless, he took out his bicycle and has been riding around the universe to see with his own eyes and reassure everyone. Lao-tzu often goes with him because he likes to keep a check on the stars in the Milky Way to see they are in the right position and properly polished, too. They either both take their bikes or ride on Lord Buddha's tandem, Lao Tse at the back of course because he's older.

When Jesus comes and walks through the forest, the flowers often ask for advice if they've muddled up their colours. The island is very peaceful even though Socrates has a motorbike but he's fixed it so that it doesn't make a noise. He uses it to ride quickly to any rainbow that needs urgent repair. Moses and Plato often play chess over a glass of mint tea. Their cottages are beside each other by the stream where it turns a corner and makes a still pool you can see your face in.

All cats know the Lavender Isle. My mother took me and my brothers and sisters there when we were silly kittens and taught us how to get to the island. It's not difficult. We played among the trees in the forest and at the stream which has lots of little bridges that go across it. The stream leads to a lake in the middle of the forest. Our mum was careful that we should not be too loud and noisy near the lake, that is to say, not disrespectful for the lake is the place – and now here comes part of our secret – where we cats gather once every ten years.

At first, we elect the two cats who will be our new king and queen for the next ten years. We have a big celebration. That's part one. In part two, the new king and queen elect the royal council, comprising twelve cats. That means an even bigger celebration. Then comes part three, the part we've been waiting for since the last meeting ten years before; indeed, you might say we have been waiting ever since anyone can remember, and our memory goes back a long, long time to when the ground was all ice and snow and we cherished our coats of fur even more than we do now.

Is it time we told old Two-Legs?

The council goes into session. Sometimes they talk for a day, sometimes the twelve of them, long-haired, short-haired, semi-long haired, those with no hair and all of the colours and patterns, all spots, stripes and irregular markings – sometimes they talk

Will the King and Queen reveal the secret?

for a week. We use the time to meet old friends, gossip a bit, hear of who's had new kittens and how many and what colour, and sometimes snooze a bit too.

The council talk in a hut by the lake. When they have come to a decision, they all come out. We all gather round. The king and queen come out last of all, paw in paw. We all miaow. With all those cats, it's a very big miaow. We are silent, watching the king and queen. If they raise their two paws above their heads in celebration, the answer is yes. If they keep their heads down and shake them, the answer is no. The question they have all been debating is a simple one: is it time we told old Two-Legs that we can talk? We can talk to him in his own language, be it English, French or double Dutch. We ask that question because we could do so much to help Two-Legs – and they could help us. But it's been decided that Mr and Mrs Two-Legs and all the Uprights are not yet aware enough. When the time comes that they can easily see the invisible then we could talk. Then – and may it come in my lifetime – we could truly work towards establishing a Parliament for Cats.

The next meeting will be in ten years. But this last meeting was a special time for me because Minnie was there. She had found her way to the Lavender Isle on the pathway I had shown her. We were very happy together. The next meeting will be in ten years but I can't wait that long to see Minnie again, not now she knows the way to the Lavender Isle. We shall be together.